The TOP SECRET Diary

of Davina Dupree

(Aged 10)

By S K Sheridan

For Bethan, Olivia and Ben

Sunday, 1st September

Hello New Diary,

My name is Davina Dupree, I'm ten and a half and I'm kind of in shock because my parents have just left me in Egmont Exclusive Boarding School for Girls. They took off in our deluxe helicopter from the middle of an enormous hockey pitch about five minutes ago and for once no one stared because arriving by helicopter is a normal thing here. A couple of girls even touched down in private jets - there's a landing strip squashed next to the tennis courts with a big sign next to it saying, 'NO Ball Games, Walking, Running or Cycling on the Runway Please'. Can you imagine!

So here I am. Abandoned. Mum shoved a brochure about the school on to my bed a couple of months ago. It had glossy photos of girls in pink, purple and white uniforms doing things like painting huge pictures, riding horses, learning to fly small aircraft (yes, really, it's that kind of school), swimming in a dolphin shaped pool with multi coloured water slides, feeding chickens in the school farm and doing gymnastics. The school building itself looks like a fairytale palace, all white marble and turrets with violet roses climbing up its walls. Quite impressive.

Mum then announced that this incredibly expensive private school would be my new home for a while as she and Dad had been assigned secret posts on an island in the Pacific Ocean. I'm never sure what their job is and they say they can't tell me for my own safety, but I think they work for the Secret Service as spies or something. They are good sorts really but we don't spend much time together. It's my wispy haired old nanny, Carrie Whepple, who usually looks after me. She's really kind and always smells of strawberry and vanilla cakes because she bakes them so much. She says they're her speciality. Mmmm, yummy.com.

But the sad news is that Carrie's just had to retire because her arthritis is so bad and she's nearly seventy, which is mega old to be working. I cried when she told me she was leaving and actually her eyes looked a bit weepy too. She gave me a photo album full of snaps of her and me from when I was a baby and she promised to write lots and come and see me when she can. Last week, I tried to teach her how to send emails but she says she doesn't trust computers and that you can't beat a good, honest, handwritten letter.

I told Mum and Dad that I DID NOT WANT TO GO TO BOARDING SCHOOL because I wanted to stay near Carrie, but they didn't listen. Instead, they just muttered things I couldn't really hear, that sounded like, 'the school will be good for you' and 'other girls your own age'.

So hey ho, here I am actually sitting on my own bed in the incredibly expensive private school, wearing the pink, purple and white uniform, with Carrie's photo album next to me. I've just looked through it again. You, dear Diary, are a present from Mum and Dad. As always, they've paid for the very best and you are have a white leather cover with a pink buckle to do you up and small yellow flowers embroidered over your front. Very pretty.com. Mum knows I like writing so she's probably hoping you'll keep me busy.

I'm kind of used to being alone anyway, because I'm an only child. I know some people think only children are spoiled brats and I suppose I am when it comes to money because my parents have got so much of it! Honestly, I don't know where they get it all from. Altogether, they own two mansions - one in the city and one in the country, a villa by the sea and four holiday apartments in different countries around the world. As well as the helicopter, they've got five vintage cars, a speed boat and a yacht. I heard Dad saying once that

he'd like to buy a private train and track one day. But what's

the point of having all that if you're never around to enjoy it? I

don't know, I really don't, I do despair of Pip and Sally. (I like to

call my parents by their first names sometimes because we

have that sort of relationship). I know they don't spoil me with

attention because Mum says when she's away (which is ALL

the time) she sometimes forgets she has a child, which is

charming isn't it? I was a bit upset when she said that actually,

but Carrie said they do love me in their own way and not to

take any notice of silly comments and that she, (Carrie), loves

me VERY much. And I love her. I hope she comes to visit soon.

At the moment I'm sitting on my bed in my 'dorm',

which is what they call a dormitory or bedroom here, although

it's not one of those horrid old fashioned ones with rows of

metal framed beds and scratchy blankets like you read about

in books. There are only two beds in this ENORMOUS room,

with purple and pink heart duvets. Along one wall there are three windows that go right up to the ceiling. Each window has purple and gold, velvet curtains draped over both sides of it, which are held in place by gold tassels. The view looks out over the school's riding stables. I can hear the ponies braying now, it's actually quite a sweet sound. I might ask if I can go riding later as I've never tried it before. I like the silver carpet that covers the floor of the dorm because it's very deep and squashy and my feet literally sink down when I stand on it. Comfy.com.

A large flat screen TV takes up the whole of another wall, which Carrie wouldn't like because she says watching too much of it rots your brain, so I might forget to mention it to her. There's a little shower and toilet room attached to the dorm, that has flashing star lights around the mirror over the sink. Pretty.com.

In the middle of the room there are two baby pink leather sofas with fluffy white cushions on them. Over to one side are two wide, wooden desks which must be for all the hard work they want us to do here. On each desk are identical new, shiny laptops, iPod's still in their boxes, fresh new folders and lots of unopened packets of pens, pencils and felt tips. Wowzers! I haven't touched any of mine yet, because everything looks so lovely in its packaging. I'm just enjoying looking at it.

The girl I'm sharing with is acting strangely. She got here first and has had her face squashed down in to her pillow ever since I arrived. She's still breathing, I checked. All I can see from her back view is that her hair is bright red and curly and her legs are extremely long and thin. When I sat on her bed and asked what her name was, she told me to go away through her pillow. How rude! Oh well, maybe she's shy or something.

Hang on, a bell just went. I think it's time for dinner.

Brilliant, I'm absolutely starving. See you later, Diary.

Monday, 2<u>nd</u> September

Hello Diary,

Yum, I had the best dinner yesterday evening. I don't know what they eat in other boarding schools but here they laid on a three course feast! I hope they do that every evening. To start, I had melon and ham with fizzy apple juice to drink. Then for the main I chose roast chicken with sweet potato mash and peas and for dessert I had triple chocolate cake with vanilla ice cream which was SERIOUSLY DELISH! We were sitting four to a table in a large dining room that has crystal chandeliers hanging from the ceiling. Each plate of food was served by a French waiter in a puffy white hat, who came zooming out of the kitchen with different dishes balanced all the way up his arms, shouting and arguing with all the other waiters at top speed. Once or twice, plates crashed to the floor and then the waiters went in to complete uproar, screaming and jumping around, with a couple actually crying. It was better than watching a play. Can you imagine!

My roommate must have been hungry because when I told her it was dinner time she lifted her head off her pillow and I saw streaky tear marks down each of her red cheeks. I pretended not to notice and started chattering away about rubbish, trying to cheer her up. She didn't talk much but she did tell me her name is Arabella Rothsbury. We ended up sitting on the same table at dinner, together with a couple of other new girls called Clarice and Cleo, who I didn't really take to as all they did was look in pocket mirrors and brush their long, swishy, blonde hair with foldaway brushes. Boring.com.

After dinner, our lovely, cosy housemistress, Mrs Honeysuckle, knocked on our bedroom door then came in to say goodnight and to find out how we're settling in. She's in charge of us for the whole of the first year. I saw the second year's housemistress, Miss Ferret, at dinner and she had a rather sharp and serious face so I'm glad we've got smiley Mrs Honeysuckle at the moment.

Arabella and I couldn't be more different and opposite. She has fiery red hair like I already said, pale skin, freckles and is as thin as a pencil. I, on the other hand, am definitely not as thin as a pencil but I'm not as fat as a tomato either, so I must be somewhere in between. My hair is golden brown, straight and so long I can sit on it. I always wear it in a plait down my back, just because it's easier like that. Arabella is quiet and serious but I like chatting. Carrie says I could talk the hind leg off a donkey although I've never actually tried it. Yet.

Arabella, who doesn't smile much by the way because she's homesick, says her favourite subject is maths. Now maths is OK but my favourite subject has got to be art, I seriously love painting pictures and want to be a famous artist when I grow up. I've been studying our time table and have seen that we've got one whole hour of art on Tuesday. At my old day school, we had the same teacher all the time who taught us pretty much everything but he wasn't that interested in art so we did it about once a month. A boy at my old school used to call me a boffin because I liked staying in at break times to do extra painting, but he didn't realise that I *have* to do extra art because I need to practise. I'll never be famous otherwise, will I?

Carrie used to work in an art gallery in London, so knows all about already famous artists, alive and dead. She's the one who first got me interested in painting. We used to paint together in the evenings when my parents were away and she said I have a 'natural talent'. Her favourite artist is a French one called Claude Monet because he painted feathery pictures of beautiful landscapes and *my* favourite is one called Vincent Van Gogh, who painted swirly pictures and went mad and chopped his ear off. Can you imagine, what a mess! They both died a while ago. Carrie says lots of artists are a bit crazy because they have so many emotions rushing round inside them which they channel to help them create amazing works of art. My absolute favourite painting by Van Gogh (you always call artists by their surnames, I'm not sure why), is one called 'Starry Night'. It is of a pretty village at night that is being looked after by the most ENORMOUS starry sky. The stars are so big they look like planets or suns and I like it because it makes me feel magical.

Gosh, I hope Arabella cheers up a bit, she's so gloomy. I do like her but it's like living with a rain cloud. We've got maths this morning so maybe that will make her smile. I'll report back to you, dear Diary, after my first, glorious art lesson.

Wednesday, 4th September

Hello again, Diary,

Well! Where do I start? I went to the art room for the first time yesterday and am pleased to report that it was as arty and colourful as I'd hoped. I was so excited when I saw it, like a chocolate addict whose been given the most delish box of chocolates in the world.

The art room's walls are painted snowflake white and it has a glass ceiling so that lots of light comes in. I looked up a couple of times during the lesson and saw birds flying - one actually went to the toilet on the ceiling above my head while I was watching – totallydisgusting.com. No one else noticed.

Two of the high walls are packed with shelves. They are full of colourful paint bottles, which stand to attention like soldiers. Piles of brushes, glue sticks, trays, clay, felt tips, cardboard and rainbow coloured pencils are squashed in around the bottles and there are rolls of bumpy material lined up under the bottom shelf - I'm not sure what these are for but they look interesting. The whole room smells divine, all painty and gluey and arty. Honestly, when I saw all this I couldn't wait to get started.

But the two art teachers – they always teach each lesson together apparently – are SO STRANGE! Not what I expected at all. They were both standing together with their hands behind their backs when we arrived and just stared at us without smiling as we came in and sat down. Because they didn't say anything and just kept eye balling us, the whole class got the giggles and for that they gave us a detention. Can you imagine how unfair!

We have quite a small class. In my old school, there were thirty of us squashed in to a room but here there are only ten to a group. There are thirty of us in the first year altogether but we're divided in to three groups and each group has been named after a precious stone. Our group is known as Sapphires and the other two groups are called Rubies and Emeralds. In our group, as well as me and Arabella, there are Cleo and Clarice, who brush their hair, file their nails and look in pocket mirrors together. Woo, what fun. Then there are the identical twins, Moira and Lynne, with their tumbly brown hair and freckly noses. They're very naughty and keep getting told off for whispering and passing notes. They love horse riding and have each brought their enormous black stallions to keep in the stables at Egmont, which is where they go whenever lessons are over. Sometimes they actually whinny like horses when they're happy. Insane.com. Melody is a very pretty girl, who sits day dreaming at the back of the class. She has chocolate coloured, shoulder length hair and big grey eyes with enormously long lashes. I've sat on the same table as her at dinner a couple of times and I like her, she's funny and she wants to be a famous actress when she grows up. Zoe wears glasses and finds learning difficult, I sit next to her in the writing class to try and help with spellings. Hannah has long legs and is very sporty, she hangs around with the older girls a lot because she has two older sisters at Egmont and Joan is very mousy and quiet. I don't know what she's like because she never says anything. Maybe I should get to know her better. When I looked around and saw us all sitting there in front of our big, white canvases, (which are stretched material blocks I've painted on before), waiting for the freaky teachers to actually start the lesson, I thought we all looked like proper artists.

But they stood and stared at us for nearly ten minutes. It was so odd.com. Miss Croaka, (they were wearing name badges), is taller than my Dad and about as wide as a bus. She has a face like a pork chop and messy black hair. When we eventually got started, she strode around the classroom, booming out instructions in her deep, manly voice. When she marched past me, I saw some beardy hairs on her chin and her breath smelt so strongly I had to turn my head away. Yuk.com.

The other art teacher, Miss Pike, is tiny. She was wearing men's clothes – a country gentleman's, green tweed dinner suit to be precise - and had an eye glass squashed in to her eye. She hardly spoke at all but when she did her words came out in a tiny, mousy squeak. What an unlikely pair!

But the weirdest thing is: neither of them are any good at art! When she actually decided to speak, Miss Croaka announced that we were going to paint self-portraits. She marched to the whiteboard with her tree trunk legs and said she was going to show us what to do. But the face she drew on the board was rubbish! It was what a three year old would draw. Actually that is insulting to young children, a three year old's drawing would have been better. All she did was draw a circle that didn't even meet, put two dots in for the eyes, a line for the nose, a wiggly half-moon for the mouth and some spikes for the hair. Can you imagine? An art teacher actually teaching us this! Well, I was shocked and there were a few gasps from around the class, (many parents would be shocked to know their high fees are paying for this kind of teaching, I'm sure), but as we'd already been given a detention for giggling nobody wanted to chance another one so we all kept quiet and got on with our work.

When I put my hand up because I needed some help with the eyes, Miss Pike came over. But do you know what she did? She rubbed out the eye I'd drawn - I'd been having trouble getting the shape of the eyelid over the eye but had put in some lashes - and she drew a dot instead. A dot! For goodness sake, they are supposed to be experts. I'm very surprised that a school like Egmont hired them in the first place. I'm quite tempted to write to Pip and Sally to ask them to complain as one of the only things I'd been looking forward to at boarding school was getting some good painting tips.

But that's not the end of it. Arabella and I were washing our painting stuff at the sink near the end of the pointless lesson when we overheard a very strange conversation between the two odd bods. They were standing in the drying cupboard next to the sink where all the wet paintings go and didn't know we were listening because they couldn't see us.

'How long have we got to put up with these wretched

kids for?' Miss Pike squeaked in her high voice. 'They're giving me a headache.'

'You know the plan, Jacinta, so don't get your knickers in a twist. There's only six weeks until blast off and we just have to be patient until then.' Miss Croaka growled back. 'Play your part properly and we'll soon reap the rewards.' Arabella and I looked at each other in amazement when she said that. We didn't understand what she was going on about, but it certainly did *not* sound good.

'I don't how those other poor idiots did this day in and day out.' Miss Pike squealed crossly. 'They must have been mad.'

'Speakin' of which.' Miss Croaka growled. 'Did you do the feedin' this mornin', Jacinta?'

'Oh darn it to the moon and back, Chris, I forgot again.'

'Are you completely useless?' Miss Croaka's voice got angrier and more rumbly. 'We agreed, alive not dead. That is really important. I suppose I'll have to do it myself after school. Where's the key?'

'Where it usually is, in my room under the notepad in the top drawer.' Miss Pinta replied huffily.

They might have gone on talking for longer if I hadn't dropped my brush and water pot in shock at that point. They came storming out of the cupboard to see who was there. It's not my fault, you don't expect to hear your teachers talking about 'alive not dead' in a lesson, do you? Arabella saved our skins by breaking in to a loud and convincing hum. She'd cheered up a lot during maths yesterday morning, because we'd been given a test to see what standard we all were and she got the highest mark in the class. She's been much smilier and talkative ever since, which is a relief, I can tell you. When

Miss Croaka and Miss Pike, or Little and Large as I like to think of them, came bombing round corner, I gave them a fake grin and started humming too. They stared at us for a minute or two with faces as angry as thunder clouds, obviously trying to work out if we'd heard anything, but we kept up our tunes and in the end they went away. Phew.com.

Arabella and I talked it over for ages yesterday evening before watching a hilarious film about talking dogs on our gigantic TV. We got all wrapped up in our fluffy duvets and drank hot chocolate with marshmallows in it! Totally delish. It's not such a hard life at boarding school actually, although I do still miss Carrie.

Anyway, basically, we both think that Croaka and Pike are highly suspect and we've decided to keep an eye on them by doing some serious detective work. I mean, what on earth were they going on about? Blast off? Reap the rewards? The feeding? Alive not dead? The Key? For goodness sake, something is so not right about that pair.

Arabella suggested we try and find the key that they were talking about, because it might give us a clue as to what they are up to. I was quite impressed with her for that. After all, if they are up to something really bad, the school ought to know. The only trouble is, Miss Pike said it's in her bedroom and all the staff have rooms in the south wing of the school, where pupils are strictly *not* allowed.

I have to go now Diary, because Mrs Fairchild - the headmistress - is going to give a talk to all us new girls in the hall.

Thursday, 5th September

Hi Diary,

Mrs Fairchild is such a lamb! She actually looks like one, with her snowy white hair all curled into ringlets against her head. Also, she has the sweetest nature. I thought she looked so tiny, standing up there on the big stage, a little white dot on a sea of polished wood, smiling away like a little child and welcoming us new arrivals to the school. I'm not sure how old she is, maybe sixty five or seventy, so she's doing really well for her age. But to be honest she *did* start laughing at a few random things and at one point she started singing and twirling around on the stage and none of us really knew what she was doing, but I thought that was rather sweet anyway.

Clarice and Cleo didn't though. They're mean girls and kept sniggering whenever Mrs Fairchild said something a bit odd, which really annoyed me and Arabella, so we poked them in the back to make them shut up. But then Clarice turn round, flicking her long blonde hair in my face and said, 'Oh look Cleo, it's the nerds,' and Cleo giggled and pulled a face at us. I mean honestly, how rude! It's not our fault that we do more work than them and get better marks, is it? If there was a 'staring in the mirror' class, Clarice and Cleo would be top of it, I'm sure. I think I'm going to suggest to Arabella that we stay out of their way from now on, because they're clearly badnews.com.

A letter arrived from Carrie today, so I wrote back at once, telling her all about Arabella, our room (I didn't mention the television), Clarice and Cleo and Mrs Fairchild. She said she's missing me a lot and that her arthritis is hurting her wrists and knees badly. She's going to come and see me in a couple of weeks, whoopee!

I'm going to meet Arabella in the lunch hall now, Diary. She says she has an idea about how we can get in to

Miss Pike's room without being caught and she's going to tell

me about it over our smoked salmon and olive multigrain pitta

breads.

Saturday, 7<u>th</u> Septmber

Oh dear, Diary,

We have to put Arabella's cunning plan in to action

this afternoon and I'm REALLY, REALLY NERVOUS! She

explained it all to me yesterday in the lunch hall – which has

canaries in gold cages hanging from the ceiling by the way,

they make one big racket while we're eating - and although it is

a brilliant plan, I'm REALLY worried in case something goes

wrong.

Basically, after lunch today, everyone in the whole

school – INCLUDING THE TEACHERS - are going to have their picture taken. It's going to be one of those enormous, long, group photographs. We have to be down by the hanging garden next to the tropical fish pond, at two o'clock sharp, just after lunch. Some men from a photo company have already arrived to build a massive stand that they are going to position all the girls and the teachers on. Arabella and I saw them putting it up while we walked back to school after feeding our baby chicks on the school farm. Each girl from Sapphires, Rubies and Emeralds has been given one of the new hatchlings to look after. Can you imagine? What a treat! Mine is sooo sweet and I've named her Lemony because, you've guessed it, she's the colour of a pale lemon. I hope I can still look after her when she's a hen.

Anyway, Arabella's brilliant and scary plan is that just as everyone is being positioned for the school photo, she's going to come over all weak and sickly. We'll ask to be excused, (I'll have to make sure I go too, to "look after her"), then when we're back in the school and sure no one's watching we'll rush over to the south wing and have a quick nosy around Miss Pike's room. The good thing is that none of the teachers or pupils are ever allowed to lock their rooms – it's a fire hazard, apparently - so what could possibly go wrong? Aggghhh!

I'll report back later, Diary, if I haven't been caught and expelled by then that is...

Saturday, 7th September (Midnight)

Diary!

I can't quite believe it, but we actually got away with it, (by the skin of our teeth), and it's a good thing too, after what we discovered.

Today, after we'd had lunch, (I could only manage a small pumpkin seed roll because I was so nervous), Arabella and I went down to the hanging garden with everybody else. It's really beautiful there, with crimson, gold, violet and pure white flowers drooping out of lots of hanging baskets that are attached to a high overhead frame. The garden smells how Turkish Delight sweets taste: totally scrummy. There's a blanket of grass underneath the hanging baskets where all of us first years sat, with Mrs Honeysuckle taking the register, waiting to be directed on to the enormous stand. All the other years in the school had their own special waiting areas.

Arabella, (who I'm now best friends with, by the way), had made a big show of feeling ill over lunch, so that everyone around us heard her moaning and groaning about wanting to be sick. She was so funny that I had to try hard not to laugh. I kept saying, 'Oh you poor thing', stroking her hair every time she collapsed dramatically across the lunch table. Melody, who was sitting with us, looked shocked and offered to fetch Matron from the Infirmary – a small hospital wing where we go if we're sick – but Arabella said not to worry - she was sure she'd feel better soon.

Clarice and Cleo, who were sitting on a table next to ours, looked beyond disgusted. It was completely fab! After listening to Arabella making nearly sick noises for the tenth time, they got up and flounced off, with Clarice saying loudly over her shoulder that she didn't want to "catch a filthy plague from a swotty nerd". I hope she hits herself in the face with her hairbrush, mean creature.

By the time the men were in the process of positioning us on the different levels of their complicated stand in height order, Arabella handily took a turn for the worse and half collapsed, saying she thought she was really going to be sick this time. I took up my acting roll and - with my heart beating so fast I could hear it in my ears - said loudly, 'Come on you poor thing, I'd better take you to the Infirmary. Stand back everyone, we're coming through.' I don't think I should ever be an actress because I sounded quite wooden but no one seemed to bat an eyelid.

We'd made sure that Croaka and Pike definitely *were* away from the south wing - we'd seen them standing silently together, giving off their weird, laser like stare, at the back of a group of teachers. Even the domestic staff were there, with the French chefs and waiters looking very dashing in their aprons and hats.

Once we were through the grand back door of the school, we raced down the corridor, turned right, raced down another corridor, skidded round the corner and came face to face with a sign that said, "SOUTH WING. TEACHER'S

QUARTERS. STRICTLY NO ENTRY TO PUPILS". We checked over

our shoulders, took deep breaths and walked past the sign.

I now know that the teachers' rooms are all off softly

lit corridors where twinkly music plays from hidden speakers.

Veryposh.com. We soon saw we'd hit a problem when we

realised that all thirty three of the teachers' doors look the

same – none have name tags or anything on them. At that

point, I honestly had no idea how we were going to find Miss

Pike's room quickly and for a moment it looked like our plan

was doomed.

We were walking up and down the first teachers'

corridor, (there are six altogether) checking each door again

and again like headless chickens, when I noticed a silvery

outline of something glowing from the door nearest me. I

stopped to look and saw that it was actually the exact shape of

Mr Drumlin the history teacher, complete with his sticking out

paunch. Thank goodness we'd a history lesson for the first time

yesterday or I wouldn't have recognised him! Someone very

clever must have painted it on with shining paint.

Cunning.com.

'Brilliant!' Arabella whispered. 'Trust this school to do

this rather than have common old name tags. All we have to

do now is find the glowing outline of Miss Pike, get in to her

room and find the key before the teachers start coming back

from the photo.'

'Oh, is that all?' I whispered with wide eyes and she

grinned. In a spilt second, we were off, working our way along

opposite sides of every corridor, stopping to stare closely at

each door in turn.

Arabella found Miss Pike's door down the sixth

corridor we trawled along. Her door was next to the one that

had the giant outline of Miss Croaka on it, which was so large,
both feet and half the head had been left off. A very strange
shape for a woman, I thought. Miss Pike's outline, on the other
hand, was so small it only took up half the door. What an ODD
PAIR! I stood on guard while Arabella knocked softly, just in
case. No one answered, so she opened the door.

As expected, the place was empty. It turns out that
the teachers don't just have one bedroom, they have a set of
rooms – an apartment really – including a lounge, bedroom,
kitchen and bathroom. Lucky things. Arabella set off across the
thick carpet towards the open bedroom door. I stood in the
doorway, constantly checking the corridor for unexpected
teachers, my head swivelling like an excited dog's on a car
journey. I listened to her rummaging through the top drawer in
the bedroom for what seemed like an hour but was probably
only five minutes.

Then she shouted, 'Wowzers, you're never going to believe this!'

'Shhh,' I replied. 'Tell me later. Just *please* hurry up.'

A few more rummaging sounds then, 'Right, I've got it,' she called. 'It's an old rusty key with a tag attached with "Bunker 37" written on it. Remember the number and we'll find out what it means. It could be our next clue to what that pair are up to. '

'I'll try,' I whispered.

Then, Bam! A door down the next corridor crashed open and I heard a voice getting nearer and nearer. A loud, *growly* voice, to be precise. My knees gave way on the spot.

'Arabella,' I called under my breath. 'I think Little and Large are coming!'

She sprinted back from the bedroom at once and

without thinking we dived out of the door, across the hallway and barged in to the apartment opposite which was also empty, shutting the door quickly. Seconds later, Pike and Croaka's voices arrived outside the room we were in. (Which turned out to belong to Mrs Turvy the music teacher and had piles of musical instruments all over the floor. I tripped over a double bass and hurt my knee.) I wondered if they'd spotted the door closing. Maybe they heard us...maybe we weren't quiet enough. We held our breaths and waited...

'Stupid school,' Croaka grumbled in her deep voice, as we heard a door handle turn. 'What a waste of time. All that fuss and nonsense about a bloomin' photo. I can't believe mad old Fairchild expected the teachers to stick around afterwards to entertain the imbeciles before tea. Surely the girls can do *something* by themselves without bein' spoon fed every step of the way.'

'I know how you feel, Chris,' piped back Pike. 'I've had enough of these spoilt brats too, but like you said the other day, we just have to be patient. It'll be worth it in the end. The important thing is, I don't think anyone noticed us slip away.'

'Listen, Jacinta, I've been thinkin'. We've only got five and a half weeks left here and by the time blast off arrives, we need to know that map off by heart, back to front and inside out.' Croaka dropped her voice. 'We can't afford to make any mistakes this time.'

'You'd better come in and we'll take another look at it then,' Pike squeaked back. We heard a door close, then there was silence. I stared at Arabella. She looked about as shocked as I felt.

'Let's get out of here,' I whispered. Arabella nodded. We let ourselves out, then tiptoed off as quickly and quietly as possible.

We'd just passed the sign that said, "SOUTH WING. TEACHER'S QUARTERS. STRICTLY NO ENTRY TO PUPILS", when Cleo and Clarice rounded the corner.

'Ooh, are the nerds being naughty?' Cleo giggled. 'I thought you'd both gone to the infirmary. Or did you just want to get out of the photo?'

'I don't blame you if you did.' Clarice sniggered. 'After all, who'd want to buy a photo with your ugly mugs ruining it?' They high fived each other then carried on trotting down the corridor towards the first year's common room, no doubt to insult more people. Arabella made a rude sign after them.

'Bad-mannered bullies,' I said loudly.

'Just forget about them. They're not worth even thinking about.' Arabella said, but she did look rather upset.

Anyway Diary, it's now midnight and we've been lying

in our beds discussing what happened all evening and I can't

BELIEVE what Arabella just told me she found in Pike's drawer

next to the key. But I'm too tired to write about it now so I'm

going to sleep, more tomorrow. Remember "Bunker 37" for

me, Diary. Good night. ZZzzzzzzzzzz.

Monday, 9th September

Greetings, Diary,

Just got back from our first whole school assembly. All

three hundred and ten of us were seated in the sort of

reclining armchairs you find in the first class sections on

planes. There were trays attached to each chair, with fizzy

limeade and biscuits waiting for each of us!

Totallyamazing.com. The lecture theatre, where all assembles take place, looks like a huge wooden cave, with a platform at the front, where Mrs Fairchild stands. (And twirls and dances, as the mood takes her). The reclining armchairs are all at different levels so us girls can see the platform at the same time.

I had a good look at all the older girls dotted around me. It's the first time I've seen them all together because usually they're floating around Egmont looking superior and busy in groups of five or six, clutching flowery folders and talking importantly. Not like us first years who still don't really know where everything is and get lost half the time.

I said hello to the serious looking girl sitting in the armchair next to mine. She had frizzy, mousy brown hair, wore glasses and turned out to be Suzie Bagshaw from the third year. She asked if I was enjoying being at Egmont and I said I was, but I was a bit disappointed with the art teaching because

42

the teachers didn't seem very good and it was my favourite subject.

Funnily enough, Suzie told me that until very recently, two DIFFERENT art teachers, Miss Cherry and Miss Wise, had taught together at the school. She said they were both BRILLIANT artists. One day, Mrs Fairchild had woken up to find hand written letters of resignation from both of them and they were never seen again. The whole school had been shocked and upset. Then Pike and Croaka just happened to turn up and walk straight in to the empty art teachers jobs. Suzie said no one liked them but then we had to stop talking because Mrs Fairchild started to sing.

When we're all together like that we look like rows of candy in our pink, purple and white uniforms. The oldest girls look so grown up, because after the fifth year, you're allowed to wear pink, purple and white business suits if you want. Until then we have to wear a white, frilly blouse, a pink hipster skirt with a silver belt encrusted with three diamonds, a purple cardigan with the school logo sewn on to it, (a hand holding the most precious stones in the world), an optional pink shawl and purple, wedged shoes with white knee length socks. It's much better than my old uniform, which was mud brown and sludge green colours.

After she'd finished her song and read out a few notices, Mrs Fairchild announced (while doing a slow waltz), that the first year nominations for two head of year prefects were now open. She said we would not be allowed to vote for ourselves, but anyone who wants to stand can start a friendly campaign to prove to the rest of the first year how trustworthy, kind and deserving of support they are. Voting will take place just before the annual Egmont Art Show that will be held on 16th October, just before school breaks up for a week's holiday. I saw Clarice and Cleo nudging each other and grinning, but I can safely say they WILL NOT be getting my vote if they stand. No way.com.

Right, I have to go now Diary, as Arabella and I are taking our favourite ponies Whiskey and Hurricane out for a slow trot so we can chat in private. Mine is Hurricane because he's not like his name, he is actually slow and relaxed. That'smysortofpony.com.

Tuesday, 10ᵗʰ September

Hiya Diary,

Right. Yesterday on our bumpy pony ride, Arabella and I talked over everything suspicious we've heard Pike and Croaka say. The naughty twins, Moira and Lynne, were out galloping madly around the paddock on their stallions, and they asked if we wanted to join them on a hack. It would have been fun as the twins are like a comedy double act – they often have our class, Sapphires, in complete stitches with their impressions of teachers - but we made our excuses as we needed to chat privately.

I'm going to list the main points we came up with here so I don't forget them:

⬚   Pike and Croaka keep talking about "blast off" – we really need to find out what this means as its obviously important to their plan.

⬚   They intend to "reap the rewards" – of what?

⬚   In the art room, Pike talked about "those other poor idiots". We think she means the art teachers who worked at Egmont before, the ones Suzie said were amazing artists. We need to find out why they left and where they are now, as it's just possible they might be able to shed some light on Little and Large's sneaky goings on.

⏺   They talked about, "The feeding". Of what? A wild animal they've kidnapped, perhaps? I wouldn't put it past them...

⏺   They want whatever they're feeding to be "alive not dead". I should hope so too or we'd have to go straight to the police.

⏺   We've found their mysterious key, now we just need to work out what "Bunker 37" means.

⏺   Croaka talked about learning a map off by heart. A map of what? Maybe the school. We have to find out.

⏺   The thing Arabella told me she found next to the rusty key was an open wallet, absolutely STUFFED with money, with a photo of a pretty, smiling lady in it. She said she didn't think there was anything else in the wallet but she didn't have time to check all the pockets. We think Croaka and Pike must have stolen it. Maybe they pick pocketed a lady in a shopping centre or something. We've decided that if we find out they're DEFINITELY criminals, we're going to tell Mrs Fairchild straight away so she can call the police and have them arrested.

We've got lots of detecting work to do and our best clue is "Bunker 37". We've decided to spy on Pike and Croaka during each art lesson, to see they let any more clues slip.

Thursday, 12th September

Oh dear, Diary!

Cleo and Clarice have started serious campaigns to get voted in as head of year prefects. It's a bit of a joke really, because they're usually so mean, but at the moment they're being sickly sweet to everyone just to get people's votes. It's all so fake.com. They even baked cupcakes this morning and offered them around in the common room but I didn't take one.

The problem is, Arabella's decided that her and I should also run for the prefect jobs, just because she hates Cleo and Clarice so much. It's a nightmare, Diary, I'm telling you! I tried to get out of it but she wouldn't give up so in the end I said I'd do it just to keep her quiet.

As you can imagine, Cleo and Clarice are being perfectly beastly to us about it. They went in to cackles of laughter when they first heard we were in the running and each time they see us they shout, "Losers" really loudly. Nasty things.

Arabella has emailed her dad, asking him to have two

campaign t-shirts made, with a photograph of us two printed

on the front, (she sent him one she took this morning just

before French, I have my eyes shut and she looks cross eyed)

with "Vote for Arabella and Davina" written in blue sequins

above our faces. Oh lawks, I hope she doesn't expect me to

wear it around school, because it would be so EMBARRASING

DOT COM!

Anyway, we have art this afternoon, so you never

know, Diary, we might learn some more about Pike and

Croaka's dirty secrets if we keep our ears and eyes open...

Friday, 13th September

OK Diary,

Action stations! Yesterday during art I overheard

Croaka – who seems to be the brains of the bunch – tell Pike to meet her in Little Pineham after school and to bring the key.

Little Pineham is the nearest village to our school and first year pupils are strictly NOT allowed to go there without a teacher. There are two supervised visits a month and I'm rather scared at the moment, because Arabella and I are about to break the rules. We're going to sneak out tomorrow, which is Saturday so no lessons, and get the bus there ON OUR OWN! WITHOUT TELLING ANY TEACHERS!

There is a reason for this madness. You see, Arabella's been to Little Pineham before - she was one of the few pupils who arrived here by train on the first day and the station is on the edge of the village. Her parents aren't as rich as mine, I don't mean that in a bad way, (at least her parent's miss her and email and phone all the time, I'd rather have not-so-rich parents that did that. Mine have only sent me one postcard so far that said, "Hello Darling, hope you're having fun. We'll be away at our undisclosed location for an undisclosed length of time but that doesn't matter now you don't live at home, does it? Lots of love Mum and Dad"), and they were trying to save money. When Croaka talked about taking the key to Little Pineham, Arabella suddenly remembered seeing a row of storerooms – which I suppose could also be called bunkers - opposite the station, each with a heavy padlock on its doors. So we're going to Little Pineham to investigate these storerooms/bunkers and see if there is a number *thirty seven*, like it says on Pike's key tag. The mystery continues...

I'm going to go now, Diary, because my hand won't write properly. It's shaking a bit because I'm so nervous.

P.S. I got a letter from Carrie today and guess what? She's coming to visit me next weekend! A week tomorrow in fact. I *so* can't wait to see her. I'm going to tell her all about

Pike and Croaka.

Sunday, 15<u>th</u> September

Uh oh Diary,

What have we got ourselves in to? The situation is a lot more serious than we thought.

Yesterday morning when I walked past the art room (without being seen of course), I saw that the charming pair, Clarice and Cleo, had roped the other charming pair, Pike and Croaka, in to giving them lots of paint and paper to make campaign posters with. Pike and Croaka did NOT look very impressed about this as it meant they had to stay in the art room for as long as Clarice and Cleo were there. (The rules say that no pupil is allowed to stay in classrooms by themselves at the weekends). This was good news for us as it meant we could go to Little Pincham without worrying we'd bump in to Little and Large.

We caught the bus in to the village, (wearing bobble hats and scarves to disguise ourselves), found the station and bunkers and guess what? There *was* a number thirty seven! It even had "Bunker 37" written on a metal plate in the middle of its large, square door. We were so excited. Needless to say, the big, fat padlock chaining the door to the wall was firmly locked and we knew where the key was – back at school in Pike's top drawer.

I heard a scrabbling sound behind the door. Arabella listened too and heard it loud and clear.

'Urgh, rats!' She said. 'I hate rats, they're all germy and disgusting. Maybe Pike and Croaka breed them. That's that mystery solved then. Yuk, let's get out of here.'

'Wait,' I said. 'I don't think its animals making that noise. Let's listen again for a minute.'

We pressed our ears next to the dirty bunker door and were very surprised when we heard a weak cough from inside. Now, I'm no animal expert but I do know that rats don't cough. The scrabbling sound seemed to be coming from the floor so I bent down to investigate and at that moment, a dirty piece of paper came sliding out of the small gap between the gravelly pavement and the door. I picked it up.

'Well, well, well,' I said, feeling like a real detective. 'It looks like your rats can write, Arabella.'

'Really? What do they say?' She leaned forwards to see. We both stared at the wobbly handwriting in shock. It said,

"We've been kidnapped. Please help us. We used to be teachers at Egmont Exclusive Boarding School for Girls until

two strange women abducted us one night. Please, please ask the police and Mrs Fairchild, the headmistress at Egmont, to free us. Thank you so much, from Katie Cherry and Harriet Wise. P.S Please take this note with you as we don't want our captors to find it. If they do they will punish us."

We stood there for a whole minute without moving, taking it all in. Then I leaned close to the door and called, 'Hello?'

'Who's there?' Came a shaky voice.

'Erm, I'm Davina,' I called through the door. 'I'm here with my friend Arabella. We're from Egmont School and we've come to, um, sort of rescue you, although we probably can't do it straight away.'

'Oh thank goodness. I'm Katie by the way, Katie Cherry.' The voice sounded emotional. 'Harriet, did you hear? Some girls from Egmont have found us. We'll be rescued soon, then we'll be able to get you to hospital.'

'Urgh,' someone groaned.

'Are you both alright?' Arabella spoke loudly. 'That groan didn't sound healthy.'

'Oh, Harriet's in an absolutely *terrible* way,' Katie said. She sounded like she might cry. 'You see –'

Suddenly, a car screeched round the corner, making Arabella and I jump.

'That's them,' Katie hissed through the door. 'That's the sound the kidnappers car always makes when they arrive. Quick, hide before they see you, or they might abduct you as well if they realise you know about us.'

What a big, fat pain. Little and Large must have escaped from the campaign poster making earlier than we'd predicted. I bet Cleo and Clarice weren't happy about that!

Before I could work out what to do, Arabella pulled me backwards and I landed on top of her behind an empty car parked in front of the next storeroom, Bunker 38. Just in time too. Before I could roll off Arabella's legs – she *does* have a few bruises on her shins today, but it wasn't my fault, it was an emergency – we heard a car swerve to a stop.

Two of its doors crashed open and the unwelcome voices of Pike and Croaka filled the air like a bad smell.

'Stand back, idiots, we're coming in,' Croaka growled. 'Jacinta, bring the peelin's.' There were some rattling sounds, a few rude words, then a door creaked open. Pike and Croaka must have walked inside because seconds later the door slammed shut and there was silence.

'Run. Fast. Now.' I said to Arabella in a low voice. 'This might be our only chance.' We pelted off down the street, towards the bus stop in the village. I was so glad to get back to school and feel safe again, but poor Katie and Harriet! They must be so miserable and Harriet sounded really ill.

So as you can see, Diary, we now know we are dealing with very serious stuff, a crisis in fact. We wanted to tell Mrs Fairchild yesterday afternoon after we got back so she could phone the police but the deputy head, Mr Longshanks, who always looks rather cross, said she was out at an all-day salsa dancing festival and that "whatever it was would have to wait till tomorrow". So we're off to see her now.

Monday, 16th September

Honestly, Diary!

I still think old Mrs Fairchild is a bit of a lamb but she's also totally crackers. When Arabella and I went to see her yesterday afternoon she had her feet up on the day bed in her study as she said she was rather sore from all the salsa-ing she'd done the day before, but she invited us to come in for a chat.

So in we went, perched on a couple of foot stools by the day bed and explained the situation as best we could, showing her Katie's note at the end.

She took her glasses off her head, stared at the note for a minute, then threw her head back and went in to peals of laughter. Honestly, I couldn't believe it!

'Oh you two nearly had me there,' she said, wiping her eyes. 'Such good larks, well done. It reminds me of the time when I was a girl at Egmont and we convinced the headmaster, Mr Crosby, that ... Oh we laughed for weeks.'

'Um, it's not a joke Mrs Fairchild, everything we just told you is true. Surely you must recognise the handwriting on that note,' I said.

'Oh stop it! That handwriting is so shaky anyone could have written it.' She was screaming with laughter again. 'Oh you two are a good tonic. I haven't laughed like this since old Bertie the caretaker got his head stuck through the cat flap when Tiddles was having a funny turn.' Tiddles is her fluffy Persian cat who none of us like because he scratches anyone who tries to stroke him.

'Honestly, Mrs Fairchild.' Arabella had a go at convincing her. 'We *know* that Katie Cherry and Harriet Wise are being held hostage in a bunker in Little Pineham because they talked to us through the door. Miss Pike and Miss Croaka are criminals.'

'But, my dear.' Mrs Fairchild chuckled. 'Katie Cherry and Harriet Wise wrote their letters of resignation themselves. I've known them for years and I'd know their handwriting anywhere. That's not to say I wasn't shocked, of course,' she

went on and a little frown appeared on her forehead. 'And a

little hurt that they didn't discuss such big decisions with me.

But it must have been what they wanted and life goes on. Did I

hear you say you'd slipped off to Little Pineham by yourselves,

you cheeky monkeys?' The frown had been quickly replaced by

a grin. 'Well I tell you what, if you run along now like good

children, we'll say no more about it.'

'But –' I began.

'Off you go, my pets,' Mrs Fairchild waved us away

with her papery hand. 'You've given me a jolly good laugh but

let me rest up now, there's good people.'

'Come on, Davina.' Arabella looked as depressed as I

felt. 'Let's go.'

So here we are, still no closer to rescuing the old art

teachers and with no idea why the new ones kidnapped the

old ones!

Arabella's having another flying lesson at the moment and I'm off to do a Thai cookery course in the food room but when we get back we're going to phone the police. Hopefully they'll be more helpful than Mrs Fairchild...

Tuesday, 17th September

Right, Diary. That's it.

I've had enough of stupid grownups, none of them are helpful. (Except Carrie of course, but she's not going to be here until Saturday and there's no point in trying to tell her about this mess until then.)

Yesterday evening, after our disastrous meeting with Mrs Fairchild, Arabella and I decided to phone the police ourselves. I mean, two poor, innocent women's lives are at stake here. They are trapped in a horrible bunker and one of them desperately ill. So using Arabella's iPhone (Carrie didn't let me have a mobile phone – she said I wasn't old enough) I phoned the emergency police number and explained everything to the gruff man at the other end of the phone. Who then had the cheek to give me an earful about wasting police time!

'Haven't you grown out of this kind of time wasting yet, young lady?' He shouted. 'You're trying to tell me that two criminal masterminds have kidnapped your teachers, locked them in a bunker and are now working as fraudulent art teachers at your exclusive boarding school? Pull the other one, it's got bells on! I should have you arrested for wasting police time, I really should. Now no more crank calls otherwise you'll find a police car turning up at your school before you can say "don't be an idiot".'

Utterly unhelpful, totally useless and extremely annoying. Arabella and I think the only thing we can do now is to take our detective work to another level and try to find a way to free the hostages BY OURSELVES.

I have to go now Diary, we have a lot to sort out.

Wednesday, 18th September

Our campaign t-shirts from Arabella's dad arrived today and she insisted we put them straight on. So I've been going around with a photo of me (with my eyes shut) and Arabella (cross-eyed) on my belly for several hours now. Feelingawkward.com.

'O.M.G.' Cleo screamed when she and Clarice came marching in to the common room to stare at us after hearing we were wearing campaign t-shirts from other members of our year. 'You can't even keep your eyes open for photographs. How sad!' They both went in to cackles of laughter then started doing impressions of how Arabella and I look in the photograph. I hadn't really wanted to be a prefect up until that moment but when I saw them smirking at me I suddenly realised that Arabella and I WOULD make BETTER prefects than them. And it made me WANT to beat them and be a prefect because I actually like most of the girls in our year, plus I do have one or two good ideas about clubs. I don't think I could stand it if Clarice and Cleo became prefects as they would become even more NASTY and UNBEARABLE than they already are, so for once I'm going to help Arabella with our campaign. That is if we have time for any campaigning while doing detective work.

We had a crisis meeting yesterday evening and have established the following facts:

▢ "Bunker 37" is a storeroom opposite the station.

▢ We now know for sure who Pike was talking about when she said "those other poor idiots". Poor Katie and Harriet.

▢ "The feeding" must have been what they went in to the bunker on Saturday to do, they've already said they want the old art teachers "alive not dead", although I'm sure Croaka told Pike to bring some peelings in to the bunker and if they're giving those women horrible potato peelings to eat I'm not surprised Harriet's ill!

▢ We believe the wallet in Pike's drawer belongs to Katie Cherry, because the photo of the pretty lady in it matches the one of her in last year's school magazine - Arabella found a copy in the library and we both had a look. She has ringletty golden hair and dimples and she looks much friendlier than Pike and Croaka. I wish she and Harriet were my art teachers instead.

⬚ We still don't know what they meant by "blast off" or "reap the rewards", or why they want to learn some map off by heart.

Our next move is to go to art this afternoon and 'innocently' ask Pike

and Croaka a few questions...goodbye for now, dear Diary...and wish me luck!

Thursday, 19th September

Well Diary,

Only two more sleeps until Carrie arrives.

Yippee! And guess what? We had a MASSIVE breakthrough in art. The only bad news is that we now have a new problem.

So yesterday, when all of Sapphire class were sitting in the art room - me next to Arabella, the twins behind us, Clarice and Cleo at the front, Melody next to Zoe at the big table in the middle so she could help her if she got stuck and Joan and Hannah by the sink - Croaka eventually stopped giving us her robotic stare and started to speak.

'You heard Mrs Fairchild mention the Annual Egmont Art Show in assembly last week.' A few of us nodded but Zoe looked blank. Melody bent over to explain it to her. 'It's being held on the 16th October at the National Gallery of Art and Design.'

Clarice and Cleo went, 'Ooh,' together and Pike glared daggers at them.

'The annoying thing is,' Croaka went on. 'We've

been told to get you horrible lot to paint a load of rubbish for us to display. It's just a show of first year's work apparently. And it's all got to be finished and dry in less than four weeks. So stop staring at me like gormless goldfish and get on with it!'

Hannah put her hand up.

'What do you want?' Croaka growled.

'What kind of things do we paint?' Hannah asked. 'When my sister Flo was in the first year, Miss Cherry and Miss Wise gave her class the theme of "Rainbow Colours", and Flo painted enormous multi coloured flowers on a canvas. It's a really good painting. Mummy hung it in our Spanish Villa.'

'I don't care what your stupid sister painted, or what your Mummy did with the canvas.' Croaka roared. 'But most of all, I don't care what those nitwits, Cherry and Wise, taught you. You've got us now, so get used to it. Paint what you like. It's bound to be a load of codswallop anyway.'

70

There were gasps from around the classroom. Hannah looked like someone had slapped her face. Zoe had tears in her eyes and to be honest, I felt like crying myself. What a waste of all the materials in the well-stocked class room. But Arabella, who didn't care much for art, was on fire. Her hand was already up and straining to be seen.

'What?' Croaka shouted, her meaty face a deeper purple than usual.

'Why did you call Miss Cherry and Miss Wise nitwits? The older girls have told us they were brilliant teachers and really kind.' Arabella said calmly. I looked at her in admiration.

'What did you say?' Croaka whispered, quivering.

'I just asked why you think Miss Cherry and Miss Wise are nitwits?' Arabella repeated.

71

'I don't have to explain myself to you, you horrible little worm.' Croaka spat. But she looked a bit flustered. Following Arabella's lead, I put my hand up.

'Why are you art teachers if you think the art we do is codswallop?' I sounded braver than I felt. Croaka opened her mouth to bawl something back at me, but Pike, who'd been signalling desperately to her co-teacher, cleared her throat.

'Ahem. We love art actually, Miss Croaka was just joking with you.' She trilled in her baby like voice. 'In fact I can't wait to hang your masterpieces in the National Gallery of Art and Design. It will be such a proud moment, the result of all our hard work as teachers this term.'

'So you two put up all our work in the gallery, do you?' Arabella asked, sounding very interested.

'Yes, just the two of us.' Pike said. 'Such a

thrilling moment. Mrs Fairchild told us that after the gallery staff leave on the evening of the 15th October, it'll just be us two left there to concentrate on getting the display ready for the following day. I honestly can't wait for that. What a position of responsibility, to be left on our own in the National Gallery.' Her eyes had developed a crafty fox like shine to them.

'Eureka.' I whispered. Arabella turned and nodded at me. She had obviously had the same thought too.

Pike and Croaka wanted to be left alone in the National Gallery of Art and Design and that could only mean one thing. THEY WERE ART THIEVES.

So now I'm feeling pretty depressed.com about the whole situation. How are two ten year olds supposed to single handedly stop a massive crime when not even their headmistress or the police believe it's even happening? I'm starting to worry that we're *not* going to be able to stop Pike

and Croaka and that they *will* rob the National Gallery of Art

and Design while Katie and Harriet starve to DEATH in that

awful bunker!

I have to go now, Diary, because I'm meeting

Melody and Hannah in the swimming pool for a water sliding

competition, but my goodness I have a lot to think about.

Friday, 20th September

Sorry Diary,

Can't write much today as I'm tidying and

cleaning our room. Carrie arrives tomorrow morning and I

want everything to look extra amazing for her.

Feelingnervous.com as I'm hoping she'll believe everything we tell her about Pike and Croaka...

Saturday, 21st September

I'm so happy, Diary!

Carrie has just left. I literally threw myself on her as soon as she'd got out of her taxi and gave her the most ENORMOUS bear hug and she gave me one back. Arabella just stood there grinning. She got on really well with Carrie, who said she approves of my choice of friend.

Had a WONDERFUL time showing Carrie around the school. We giggled so much at all her, "Oh my's" and "Well, really's", as we showed her the runway, the hanging garden, the stables and the swimming pool with waterslides. She tutted when she saw the giant flat screen TV on our bedroom wall, but her eyes were smiling at me.

We took her for tea and scones in our chandelier lit dining room, (which she declared to be "very posh") and while we were eating the cherry scones with piles of whipped cream and strawberry jam, Arabella and I told Carrie all about Pike, Croaka, Katie and Harriet.

'Now, you're not pulling my leg are you, girls?' Carrie asked sternly when we'd finished, looking me straight in the eye.

'No Carrie,' I said, deadly serious. 'I promise, everything we've told you is the total truth.'

She stared at me for half a minute more, then said, 'I believe you. You're telling the truth, I can see it in your eyes. Anyway, you always were a lousy liar, young Davina, and that's not a bad quality to have.'

Arabella and I grinned at each other. Phew! At last, a grown-up who was taking our emergency seriously.

'Pike and Croaka,' Carrie said as she piled jam on another scone. 'Now why do those names sound familiar?' She stared in to the distance, thinking while she was chewing. 'No,' she said after devouring the whole scone and licking her lips. 'It's no good, my memory's not as quick as it used to be. It might come back to me later.'

'What shall we do about poor Katie and Harriet, Carrie?' I asked, sipping my Darjeeling tea. 'We can't just leave them stuck in that dirty old bunker – after all, Harriet is seriously ill - but the police don't believe us.'

'What's wrong with Harriet?' Carrie asked.

'We're not sure,' Arabella said. 'Pike and Croaka arrived before Katie could tell us.'

'Hmm,' Carrie said. 'I don't suppose there's any point in me going straight to the police and telling them everything. They'll probably just think I'm a batty old lady who's off my rocker - if they didn't believe you there's no reason they'll believe me.' She thought for a moment, and then said, 'Right. I'll tell you what we'll do. Do you remember my friend, Hugh Broderick, Davina?'

'I think so,' I replied, the memory of an old man with white tufty eyebrows and a kind smile coming in to my head.

'It just so happens that he's a retired policeman,' Carrie went on. 'He used to be quite high up in the force, as I remember, got to detective level I think, and he still helps train a lot of the younger policemen. He's the man we need to speak to and he knows me well enough to believe everything I tell him.'

'Brilliant!' I said. 'I knew you'd help us, Carrie.'

'Hang on a minute,' she said. 'Hugh's abroad at the moment. He and his wife have gone on holiday to Italy, although I'm not sure which part so I have no way of getting in touch with him. They are due back in a couple of weeks and as soon as I know they're home I'll go round and tell him everything. There's no way I'm going to allow two pathetic art thieves to steal from our national collection if I can help it. No way, no how. But things have to be done properly or we'll end up causing trouble rather than fixing it.'

'TWO WEEKS?' I shrieked, quite loudly in fact, making Moira and Lynne – who were entertaining their mum (who, like them, was wearing jodhpurs) with loud tales of the practical jokes they'd played on teachers – turn and stare. 'Katie and Harriet can't go on living in that prison for another two weeks!'

'Calm down my dear.' Carrie said, soothingly. 'I'll pop by the bunker every couple of days and slide some nourishing food under the door. You said there was a bit of a gap there. Little Pineham is only two bus rides away from my house.'

'You're an angel Carrie,' I said, meaning it.

'Oh give over,' she said gruffly, but I could tell she was pleased.

It was horrible saying goodbye to her again, Diary, and I do have to admit to you that I had a bit of a cry. But Arabella cheered me up by doing impressions of how Cleo and Clarice look when they swish their hair and look in their mirrors. I'm glad I've made such a good friend here at Egmont.

Carrie's going to visit me again in a couple of weeks and hopefully she'll have spoken to that retired detective chap by then.

I have to go now, Diary, because Arabella and I are going to watch our favourite programme, "Spy of the Week".

Monday, 23rd September

Hello Diary,

I had a complete brainwave yesterday! I suddenly realised that just because Pike and Croaka are criminals who are rubbish at teaching art, it doesn't mean that the first year have to miss out on producing their best possible paintings for the Annual Egmont Art Show. So I went off to see old Mrs Fairchild again, taking Arabella with me for moral support, and asked if some of us in the first year could have extra time in the art room to prepare for the art show. Luckily she agreed.

'Oh you two are funny,' she said as she practiced yoga on a mat in the middle of her study floor. She can bend her legs quite high for someone her age. 'One minute you're trying to have the art teachers arrested and the next you want to spend extra time doing their subject! Well I think it's a splendid idea. I'll ask Bertie the caretaker to give you a spare key to the art room and you can pop in and doodle away to your heart's content. After all, the paintings in the show are usually of an exceptionally high standard and some very important people come to view them.' Mrs Fairchild's twinkly eyes turned serious for a minute. 'Royalty and state leaders from around the world will come and see the art show and so will various diplomats, politicians and celebrities. Some will come because their daughters already attend Egmont and they want to support the school. Others will be *thinking* of sending their daughters here and will visit the art show to see proof that in all subjects we teach children to the highest possible standard.

82

It would be an utter disaster for Egmont's reputation if the school's art show was not well thought of. But I'm sure it will be,' she said, her smile and twinkly eyes returning. 'Now run along and find Bertie and ask him to come and see me, there's good people. I don't think we need to bother Miss Pike and Miss Croaka with this arrangement, do you? I can tell I can trust you two to take good care of the art room by yourselves.'

'She's not as bonkers as she makes out, is she?' Arabella muttered as we trotted off down the corridor.

'Nope,' I smiled. 'I think underneath it all she might be rather clever.'

Mrs Fairchild kept her word and yesterday evening Bertie brought us our very own key to the art room. Can you imagine!

I have to go now, Diary, because Arabella and I have called a meeting about the Annual Egmont Art Show for all first years and it begins in the common room in ten minutes.

Tuesday, 24<u>th</u> September

What a result, Diary!

Yesterday evening, twenty eight first years were waiting for us in the common room. I'd mentioned our idea to Moira and Lynne earlier in the day and they both said they hated art and wouldn't be turning up, which didn't surprise me. But still, the rest of the year had turned up to see what we had to say. Including – unfortunately - Cleo and Clarice.

They sniggered their way through Arabella's speech while she explained that we were sick of Pike and Croaka spoiling each art lesson and that we'd like a chance to create the best paintings we can for the art show. They rolled their eyes and snorted when she said we'd asked Mrs Fairchild if we

could do extra art in the evenings and they called out 'nerds'

when I stood up and asked if anyone fancied joining us

sometimes to do a bit of extra painting.

'As if anyone would want to hang out with you two

swotty saddo's!' Clarice yelled.

'Erm, actually, I would.' Melody said. I could have

hugged her. 'I think it's a great idea, Davina.'

'Yeah, me too,' said a girl called Rochelle from

Emerald class.

'And me,' Linda from Rubies called. 'Everyone in my

class hates Miss Croaka and Miss Pike. It's about time we

painted something our parents would be proud of.'

'I'll come sometimes, when I don't have hockey

practice,' Hannah said. 'Good on you both for arranging this. I'll definitely vote for you guys to be head of year prefects.' There were even a few murmurs of agreement when she said that Diary, can you imagine!

This was all too much for Cleo and Clarice to take, and they stormed out, muttering something about not wanting to hang out with a bunch of losers.

I'm now off to my first extra painting session WITHOUT Croaka and Pike, so I'll see you later Diary.

P.S. Carrie phoned Arabella to say that her first food delivery had been successfully pushed under the bunker door for Katie and Harriet. She managed to shove through a flat piece of cheese, a few slices of bread, some sliced fruit and a few small cupcakes, which have *got* to be more tasty than old peelings.

Wednesday, 25th September

Uh oh, Diary,

I think there's trouble afoot. After hearing that we had so much unexpected support from the other first years and especially after hearing a few of them say they'd vote for us to be prefects, Clarice and Cleo have declared war against us. Melody told me that they're spreading rumours, telling people that we talk and laugh about other first years behind their backs, (which is *so* wrong because that's actually exactly what *they* do!) and that although we seem nice we're really two faced and mean. I mean, HOW UNFAIR.COM! Arabella says they're pathetic and that no one will believe them. I just hope she's right.

It's really difficult waiting for Carrie's detective friend, Hugh Broderick, to get back from his holidays before we can help Katie and Harriet. I hate to think of them stuck in that dark, cold bunker. But at least they have Carrie now and I feel better knowing she's keeping an eye on them.

I'm very proud of the paintings we started yesterday evening by ourselves. Arabella and I had already looked around the art room before the other first years came to join us, so we felt read to help with a few ideas up our sleeves.

'Look,' I said to Rochelle, when she said she was stuck for ideas. 'In this book, "Sparkle Flowers", it shows you how to paint a beautiful, large flower with green leaves and how to decorate it with sequins and glitter. Why don't you try that?'

'Thanks,' she said. 'I will. I've never seen that book before. I don't think Miss Croaka and Miss Pike ever showed it to us.'

'I'm not surprised, Rochelle.' I said, shaking my head.

'Someone had stuffed all the art books in to an old box at the back of the cupboard. Arabella found them when we were looking around the art room for ideas earlier.'

Arabella showed Ashvini from Emerald class a book about painting ocean pictures. I saw them looking at prints of colourful fish, palm trees on sand islands and sunken treasure. Then Ashvini chose a bottle of aqua-marine paint and started to paint curly wave patterns on her canvas.

After thirty minutes, everyone was stuck in to their paintings. Hannah was doing a portrait of her mum, looking at a photograph to get a good likeness. Zoe was painting a pattern on her large canvas, zig zagging with red, swirling with green and painting stars in gold. Two girls from Rubies had decided to share a giant canvas and they were painting a picture of a secret garden on it, drawing it carefully on in pencil first, before they colouring it with paint. It was all so artistic.com!

The moment I'd been looking forward to most had arrived. It was time to start my own painting and I knew exactly what I was going to do. It was an idea I'd come up with a while ago, something that might cause problems for Croaka and Pike. I hadn't told Arabella in case she told me it was a stupid idea – I already knew it might get me in to trouble. Best of all, I was going to paint it in the swirly, big brush-stroked style of my favourite, one-eared artist: Vincent Van Gogh, exactly like he did in "Starry Night".

Once I'd started painting, I couldn't stop. It was like I was in a dream. One by one the other first years said goodbye and left, saying they'd come back the next evening, but I just carried on painting. Arabella tried to talk to me but I couldn't give her a sensible reply so she gave up and went to sleep on a desk – it didn't look very comfortable as one of her legs and both arms were hanging off the sides.

I painted all night, dabbing, mixing colours, smearing paint with my hands and creating a daring picture that I was very pleased with but that I knew Croaka and Pike would HATE. And they're going to see it for the first time in art tomorrow...

I have to go to sleep now Diary, as I'm very, very...zzzzzzzzz

Friday, 27th September

Panic stations, Diary!

Croaka and Pike had already seen my painting by the time Sapphire class got to the art room yesterday afternoon. They were totally insane with anger.

'Wowzers!' Moira shouted when she and Lynne came galloping in. The room was alive with brightly coloured canvases and finally looked how an art room should. I felt a stab of pride for my fellow first years, they'd done themselves proud.

'These lot are brilliant, Davina. Which one is yours?' Moira asked.

'That one over there,' I said, pointing to one in the corner and going red at the same time. Moira's mouth fell open.

'The one that looks like the inside of an art gallery, with the rows and rows of paintings in gold frames all over the walls?'

'Yes,' I said, aware that Pike and Croaka had come to stand next to me, very close indeed.

'But what's that in the corner of it, is it a person?' Moira asked, leaning forwards to see.

'It's an art thief.' Her sister Lynne announced. 'Look, he's wearing a balaclava with just his eyes showing and Davina's set the painting at night time because you can see the moon and stars through the window. Isn't that right, Davina?'

'Erm, yes.' I was hardly able to get the words out now that Croaka and Pike were so close. I was finding it difficult to breath. To be honest, I was rather proud of my painting - it showed how I imagined Egmont's art exhibition would look inside the National Gallery of Art and Design. I'd been to a few galleries before and they were all very grand, with enormous paintings in gold and silver frames hung round velvet curtained windows. In my painting, the gallery walls were a deep red colour which went together nicely with the gold frames. I'd copied the first years' actual paintings inside the frames, so that Rochelle's glittery flower was hung next to the secret garden picture, and Ashvini's ocean painting hung next to Zoe's bold pattern. And Lynne was right. I'd painted in a shifty looking art thief in the shadows, just about to steal a painting. You see, I thought if Pike and Croaka suspected that their plan was no longer a secret, it might just scare them in to calling off the whole thing. It was a bit of a risk, and one that had seemed like a better idea in the middle of the night when Pike and Croaka weren't standing right next to me.

'Look, the art thief's bag is on the floor next to him,' piped up Zoe, who was the nearest to my painting. 'It's full of the tools he's going to take a painting off the wall with. It's really good, Davina. I didn't know you were so good at art.'

'Urgh.' I gurgled.

'Yes Davina,' mimicked Croaka. 'I didn't know you were so good at art either. Tell me,' she said, bending down so that her giant slab of a face was level with mine, 'what gave you the idea to paint that, very particular, piece of work?'

'I-I-I wanted to see what you thought of it,' I stammered.

'You know something, don't you Davina?' Pike hissed in my ear, just loud enough for me to hear. 'Something that little girls have no business knowing.'

'I don't know anything about you,' I said loudly, sounding braver than I felt. 'I don't know what you mean. What kind of thing d-d-do you think I know?'

'It's a very unusual painting that Davina has done, isn't it Miss Croaka?' Arabella asked, coming to my rescue. She hadn't seen the finished painting until then, because she'd somehow been sleeping soundly on her desk when I'd finished it. I'd had to half guide, half carry her back to our room, just as the sun began to rise and the birds warmed up their voices.

After staring at it with her mouth wide open after we first came in to the art room, then raising her eyebrows at me as though I was mad, I knew she got it. She understood that we had to try and crack Croaka and Pike's plan in any possible way, even if it that way was a bit stupid and dangerous.

'I mean, it clearly shows the Annual Egmont Art Show, but I'm wondering why Davina's included a thief about to steal a painting...Do you think that sort of thing could ever really happen?'

Croaka and Pike rounded on her, giving me a bit of breathing and thinking space. The rest of Sapphire class were all sitting up, looking interested and a bit worried. The tension in the room was so thick you could have cut it with a knife. Even Cleo and Clarice were listening, hair brushes hanging from their hands.

'You know something you shouldn't too, don't you

girl?' Pike squeaked loudly. 'Right, that's it. I've had just about enough of you meddling kids. Chris, it's time for Plan B.'

Arabella and I looked at each other in alarm. What was Plan B? We weren't prepared for that one. But I noticed that the look on Croaka's face had turned from anger to cunning. She turned back to me and stared with narrowed eyes, like a cat watching a mouse.

'Hold your horses, Jacinta, dear. I rather think darlin' Davina might have dealt us a new trick. Which I'll explain to you after class,' she said loudly before Pike could protest. Pike looked sulky but shut her mouth and stomped around the classroom in a bad mood for the rest of the lesson.

As usual, they taught us nothing, so we just got on with what we liked, which in most cases was getting paintings ready for the Annual Egmont Art Show. Now that we'd found the helpful art books that Pike and Croaka had no doubt hidden, thinking them useless, we could teach ourselves.

But I wasn't having fun at all because Croaka stayed very close to me all lesson and I had a horrible feeling she wasn't going to let me go at the end.

I was right. After the rest of Sapphire class had filed out when the blast of Mozart played through the loud speaker (the sign that the lesson had ended), Croaka, who'd been guarding me like a Rottweiler with anger problems, slammed her fleshy hand on top of mine. I was thankful to see that Arabella was refusing to move, despite Pike trying to get her out of the door.

'So, Dupree,' Croaka growled. 'It's time to come clean. What's your paintin' about? You see, Miss Pike and I can't help thinkin' you might know about a little secret we have and if you do, it's VERY important that you tell us. Because if you don't... Well. Let's just say, things could turn extremely unpleasant for you.'

'Leave her alone, you big bully,' Arabella was red in the face.

'Stop her from talkin', Jacinta.' Croaka snarled. 'It's this one I want to hear from. Come on, don't be shy Davina. We usually can't shut you up. Why don't you tell us why you painted a thief about to steal a painting. Talk us through what gave you that particular idea. Step by step, if you don't mind.'

I was pretty sure I wasn't going to say anything as up until that point I hadn't been sure what *to* say. I'd just wanted to shock the two of them a bit, give them a clue that we knew what they were up to just in case it scared them in to stopping. But that's as far as my plan had ever got. But as I stared in to Croaka's piggy little eyes, I felt an angry red mist arrive in my head.

'Because,' I said, 'I don't want YOU TWO stealing

anything from the National Gallery of Art and Design when you're supposed to be putting up OUR SCHOOL ART SHOW. I'm SICK of the rubbish art lessons you give, I'm sick of you being mean to everyone, but most of all I'm SICK of knowing that you two bullies are keeping the LOVELY art teachers who *should* be teaching us, Katie and Harriet, in a disgusting bunker near Little Pineham station, feeding them on old peelings. I wish you'd never come here because you've COMPLETELY RUINED MY FAVOURITE SUBJECT!' I felt madder than I'd ever felt before and I couldn't stop shaking. Pike, Croaka and Arabella were all staring at me with their mouths open. Arabella did not look happy.

Croaka recovered herself quickly.

'Well, well, well. Aren't you a good, little detective, Davina Dupree. A proper superhero, in fact. You've even found yourself a trusty sidekick.'

'Hey, who are you calling a sidekick?' Arabella yelled. 'We're *partners* in solving crimes, aren't we Davina?'

'We certainly are,' I said, giving my best friend a grin. Now that I'd had my say, my anger was beginning to flow away and in its place, I was sorry to find, was terror. 'Anyway, it was great to have such an honest chat with you guys but if you'll excuse us we have another lesson to go to. Madame De Guise gets mad if anyone is even a minute late.'

'If you think you're going anywhere after –' Pike began but Croaka laid a hand on her arm and said,

'Of course Davina. You two run along to French and send our apologies to Madame De Guise. Just say you were helping us solve a little puzzle. We'll be seeing a lot more of you later, I'm sure.'

We got out of that classroom as fast as we possibly could, Diary, and I can tell you that I DEFINITELY did NOT like the crafty look in Croaka's eyes as we left. We know she's up to something but we can't think what. Arabella says she's surprised they let us out of that classroom at all after what I told them, (she's not very pleased with me about that actually, says I've probably landed us both in a whole heap of trouble.)

Anyway, Diary, I've got to go now because earlier Mrs Fairchild announced – over the school loud speaker system – that we were going to have a surprise assembly and it starts in fifteen minutes.

Sunday, 29th September

Help, Diary!

It looks like Arabella was right, I have landed us both in a whole heap of trouble, as we found out during the surprise assembly...

Basically, Mrs Fairchild told us – in between sit ups and squat jumps – that Pike and Croaka had gone to see her on Friday evening with a shocking announcement. They'd explained that the director of the National Gallery of Art and Design, Mr Cerise, had phoned them up straight after they'd taught Sapphire class and asked if the Annual Egmont Art Show could be moved from the 16th October to the 1st October, which is in two days time: this coming Tuesday.

Arabella and I are both quite sure that Little and Large somehow managed to persuade Mr Cerise to change the date to the 1st October because of what I told them. They simply don't want to be stopped from thieving loads of priceless paintings so they're going to do whatever it takes to keep their plan going. I can't help feeling surprised that so far they haven't kidnapped Arabella and I and shoved us in Bunker 37 with Katie and Harriet. We are always looking over our shoulders to check they're not behind us. Just in case. I have a nasty feeling about all this. Feelingverynervous.com.

I'm walking around with you, Diary, tucked up my shirt, disguised with the optional school pink, glittery shawl. So far no one's noticed. I've written information in you that I'm sure Pike and Croaka would love to read if they could get their hands on you. Also, I always have a pen stuck behind my ear, just in case I need to write anything.

Things have got worse with the Clarice and Cleo situation. They're so obsessed with dirtying our names that they've even gone to the trouble of forging some typed notes, apparently by us, that said rude things about our classmates. Hannah showed me one about her, looking very upset.

'Did you really write this about me, Davina?' She asked, handing me a bit of paper with typing on it. 'Cleo said she saw it fall out of your bag and that she picked it up ready

to give back to you, but when she read it she thought I had a

right to know what you're really like.'

I read the note. It said, "Arabella, you were right

about Hannah. She does have the biggest nose in the class,

what a whopper! Love Davina."

'No I certainly did not write that.' I said, very shocked.

'I would never say anything horrible like that about you,

Hannah. I think your nose is lovely. Cleo must have written it

herself.'

'Hmm, I can't think of any reason she'd do that,'

Hannah said without smiling, before she walked away. Arabella

said Moira and Lynne had showed her a similar note about

them and said they weren't going to vote for us after all

because they'd realised we were two-faced. Things are going

from bad to worse. I mean, how can people believe we would

really write that kind of stuff?

I have to go now Diary, I'm too jumpy to write any more and anyway, Arabella and I are holding a crisis meeting. Things are critical.com.

Monday, 30th September

OK, Diary, here's the deal:

This afternoon we were kidnapped and I'm not even joking. Arabella and I had just finished our SECOND crisis meeting under the hanging garden. No one was around which we'd expected as it was raining a bit and we'd just agreed that we needed to phone Carrie again, (she didn't answer her home phone yesterday for some reason and she refuses to own a mobile one), and explain the new developments to her. We wanted to ask her to go straight to the police station, even if her friend Hugh Broderick was on holiday, and CONVINCE the police about the art robbery. If she didn't answer again, we'd have to try and tell Arabella's parents. Things had gone far enough.

But we didn't have time to do any of this. Just as we walked underneath a very long piece of ivy, two pairs of hands shot out from behind a pillar that holds part of the hanging garden in the air, and clamped themselves over both our mouths. We were then dragged backwards for what seemed like half an hour, our feet bumping over the wet grass, until we reached Croaka's car. Pike opened one of the back doors and told us to climb in or there would be trouble. So we did, we honestly didn't have much of a choice.

I thought they'd take us to Bunker 37, but instead, Croaka drove for ages and ages with Pike next to her, while we rattled around in the back of her stinking car with no seat belts

to protect us from her TERRIBLE driving. Around us, there was

mouldy food stuck to the seats, old drink bottles rolling around

on the floor and half a burger falling out of a plastic box

between us that slopped on to me when she screamed round a

corner. Honestly Diary, it smelt so disgusting I nearly threw up.

Eventually we arrived somewhere – at first I didn't

have a clue where – in the dark. Croaka's car clock said it was

half eleven at night. They told us to get out, took Arabella's

iPhone out of her pocket and made sure I didn't have one,

then frog-marched us towards a large, modern looking

building. (They didn't find you, Diary, as no one thought of

looking behind my shawl.) Most of its walls seemed to be

made from shimmery glass and it was very wide.

Anyway, with Croaka holding on to me and Pike

clutching Arabella, we climbed up an enormous flight of steps at the front of the building towards a large, glassy door, lurching from side to side like a group of drunk old men.

'I know what this place is,' I whispered across to Arabella as I stared through the door. 'I recognise it now, I've seen it in one of Carrie's art books. It's the National Gallery of Art and Design. They've got a painting of a field by Claude Monet, Carrie's favourite artist, hanging in the entrance hall. Look.'

'Well done, Detective Davina,' Croaka sneered, grabbing my arm even tighter. 'This *is* the National Gallery of Art and Design and for one night only, it belongs to me and Jacinta. It was easy to get the director, Mr Cerise, to move the date of the Annual Egmont Art Show. I just phoned him up and explained that Mrs Fairchild, the head at Egmont, was desperately ill with only a few weeks to live and really wanted to see one last art show before she died. Jacinta phoned him up separately, pretendin' to be Mrs Fairchild's doctor and confirmin' everything I'd told him. He said, "Oh poor Mrs Fairchild, she's always been such a great supporter of the arts," and agreed at once. Easy as pie, when you know how.'

'You're not nice,' Arabella said. 'Fancy saying something like that about Mrs Fairchild. I hope she goes on living for one hundred more years at least.'

'Quiet, you little worm,' Pike snapped.

'You do realise,' I said. 'That when Mrs Honeysuckle our housemistress comes round to check we're all in bed, she'll realise we're not there and call the police.'

'You do realise,' mimicked Croaka. 'That we've already told Mrs Fairchild you were both very keen to help us put up the art display at the National Gallery, bein' such incredibly arty pupils. They're not expectin' you back at Egmont until late tomorrow evenin' and by then it'll be too late.' I swear she let out a real cackle at that point.

'Too late for what?' Arabella asked.

'Oh, you'll find out.' Pike jeered.

By then we were all soaked by the splattering rain. Croaka took a pearly white card with numbers all over it out of her pocket and slipped it through a device on the glassy door. Something inside the door clicked and it slid open.

'Kind Mr Cerise gave it to me earlier,' she said boastfully, flicking a load of light switches then pushing me forwards. 'We had to drive all the bloomin' rubbish over this morning that you kids have been painting – Mrs Fairchild was watchin' us load it all in to my car or we wouldn't 'ave bothered – and he gave it to me then. Said all the gallery staff would be out of our way by this evening so we could get on with the time honoured tradition of putting up the Egmont Show. As if.' Croaka and Pike looked at each other and sniggered.

They marched us through the entrance hall, past the golden field of poppies by Monet, then down corridor after corridor, past a few famous paintings I recognised and loads that I didn't, until we got to a door that had a yellow and blue sign on it.

'Cleaning cupboard,' Arabella whispered.

Croaka used her pearly white magic card to unlock the cupboard door. Then they pushed us inside, a little bit harder than necessary in my opinion, then slammed the door shut. We heard their horrible laughter fade in to the distance as they went off to steal paintings.

It was pitch black.

'Right. Let's get out of here,' came Arabella's strong voice. I could feel her stand up and stumble around.

'Aha, I've found the light switch,' she said, flicking it on. I looked around.

We were squashed amongst vacuum cleaners, bottles of cleaning stuff and brooms. There were lots of shelves above our heads, piled with spray cans and dusters. There was an inside door handle and I tried it with all my strength, but as expected, it was firmly locked.

'Now what are we supposed to do?' Arabella said crossly. She kicked a pile of crumpled boxes that were in front of her and they tumbled over. Things spilled out everywhere and soon I was surrounded by old sponges, cloths and dusters. I noticed something shimmering under a cloth and leaned forward to pick it up.

'Arabella, look!' I said. 'It's a pearly white card, exactly like the one Croaka used to open all the doors.'

'Good find, Davina.' She said, leaning over to have a

closer look at it. 'Hmm, it's a bit chipped round the edges.'

'Yes,' I said. 'It must have belonged to the cleaners. They probably need to open all the doors in the building so they can clean everywhere. Maybe they chucked it in that box and forgot about it when they were given a newer one.'

'The question is, will it open this door, or is it too broken?' Arabella asked.

'Only one way to find out,' I said. I turned back to the door. It had the same device on this side as it did on the other, a little box with a narrow gap down one side of it. I took a deep breath, then whooshed the card through the gap. There was a pause. Then a click!

'Nice one,' Arabella grinned, carefully picking her way over the floor. I turned the handle as quietly as possible, just in case. and in a minute we were standing in a dark corridor full of enormous shadowy paintings. We looked at each other.

'Now what?' I whispered.

'Now we find a telephone and call Carrie. The sooner the police get here the better.' Arabella whispered back.

I nodded. My heart was hammering loudly as we stood in the corridor, with no idea which way to go. It was dreadfully important that we found a phone before Croaka and Pike found us. I knew that at some point they'd come back and check on us and find an empty cupboard. And who knew what would happen then. Scary.com.

Anyway Diary, that's where we are now, still in the corridor. I had a chance to write in you while Arabella looked for a phone in every room that's off this corridor. She's coming back from the last one now, shaking her head, so I must go. I can hear some muffled tapping noises and I think we should find out what they are. Wish us luck...

Some time in the middle of the night between

Monday 30th September and Tuesday 1st October...

So we now know the tapping noises were Croaka and Pike trying to chip a large gold frame off the wall in the Orange Room because we saw them. (All the rooms in the gallery are named after different colours – very imaginative.)

We crept along the corridors, past the Pink and Green Rooms, through the Purple Hall and up to the door of the Orange Room. This was where the noise was coming from. The door was open a bit and we stared through the crack to see the AWFUL sight of Croaka standing on a ladder, being supported by Pike, hammering a sharp spike behind one corner of an enormous gold frame then trying to pull it off the wall. They mustn't have been able to steal the paintings without getting the frames down first and I was glad to see they were finding it very difficult. And do you know what painting they were trying to steal first? "Starry Night" by Vincent Van Gogh. MY FAVOURITE PAINTING BY MY FAVOURITE ARTIST! Seethingwithanger.com.

'I think I saw a phone back there in an office we just passed,' Arabella whispered. 'Come on.'

So we tiptoed back and found she was right. In an office marked 'Events Organiser' there was a phone sitting on the corner of the desk. I rushed over, picked up the receiver, tapped the only phone number in the world that I knew off by heart (I don't know my parents mobile numbers as they don't tend to answer them, being on secret missions in far off countries), and waited, biting my nails, listening to Carries phone ringing and ringing.

'Please pick up. Pleae pick up,' I whispered over and over again.

Just as I was about to put the receiver down again, feeling very depressed...

'Hello?' Came Carrie's crackly, tired voice.

'Carrie!' I shouted in relief. Arabella put her finger to her lips.

'Davina, is that you?' Carrie said, yawning. 'What on earth are you ringing for at this time of night?'

'Sorry Carrie, but please listen. I'm going to try and explain everything but we don't have much time. You see, earlier on today, Pike and Croaka kidnapped us and locked us in a cupboard in the National Gallery of Art and Design.'

'They did what?' Carrie shrieked, suddenly sounding very awake. 'Are you alright, Davina?'

'Yes fine, we escaped. After they found out we were on to them they convinced the director at the National Gallery to move the starting date of the Egmont Art Show to tomorrow, by saying Mrs Fairchild was desperately ill and wanted to see one last art show before she died.'

'The absolute rotters, that's outrageous!' Carrie sounded very angry. 'Where are they now?'

'Erm, at the moment they're trying to knock Vincent Van Gogh's "Starry Night" painting off the wall so they can steal it,' I said.

'Absolutely disgraceful behaviour,' Carrie spat. 'Right Davina, here's what we'll do. Mrs Peverell from the grocery shop told me that Hugh Broderick and his wife Marjorie flew back from Italy yesterday – they came back a bit earlier than expected because Marjorie got food poisoning and wanted to go home - which is bad news for her but good news for us. I'm going to go round there now, I don't care if it *is* the middle of the night – this is an emergency – and tell him everything. He's a good man, he'll jump in to action. Meanwhile, I want you two to find a *really* good hiding place – somewhere those two scoundrels won't find you - and stay there until they've been arrested and it's safe to come out. Is that understood?'

'Yes Carrie,' I whispered, feeling relieved. 'Good luck with Hugh.'

'Good luck yourself,' she said. 'Now go and find that hiding place.'

'What did she say?' Arabella whispered as I placed the receiver back ever so quietly.

'She said we've got to- ' I turned and stopped. Pike was standing in the doorway looking madder than a cat in a catnip factory.

'Chris!' She yelled. 'The little worms have escaped.'

'Run!' Arabella yelled. I didn't need telling twice. We

joined hands and ran towards Pike in unspoken agreement, bashing her out of the way as we pelted through the doorway. She tried to grab us but fell sideways as we ran on. A deep roar and pounding footsteps that sounded worryingly close came from the Orange Room. Croaka was obviously not a happy bunny.

We sprinted down corridor after corridor, past priceless paintings from around the world. A terrible stitch started in my side but somehow I kept going. We didn't know where we were going, we just ran and ran. But Pike was gaining on us and from the growly insults being yelled, Croaka wasn't far behind. What with all the coughing and spluttering, neither of them sounded very fit.

Suddenly, we hit a dead end. The corridor we were on just ended with a wall. We flattened ourselves against it, as Pike and Croaka wheezed and spluttered to a standstill.

'I've had just about enough of you two.' Croaka's eyebrows were knitted together with anger. 'Jacinta, grab them. Their luck just ran out.'

Pike stepped forward and took Arabella and I roughly by the arm. But just as she started to drag us towards Croaka, a familiar voice echoed down the corridor.

'Unhand them this minute, Miss Pike.' I looked up and saw the most welcome but unexpected sight of Mrs Fairchild. This time, the tiny old lady wasn't dancing, twirling or doing yoga. She looked deadly serious – rather cross in fact - as she walked towards us, eyes flashing. Pike loosened her grip on us, but Croaka laughed.

'How exactly are you going to stop us doing exactly what we want, old lady?' She jeered. 'Hit us over the head with your handkerchief?' Croaka tuned to grin at Pike. That was her big mistake because while her head was tuned, Mrs Fairchild, who'd arrived next to the art thieves, hitched her skirt up, crouched down, twisted, then whopped Croaka in the stomach with her foot – VERY HARD. And she was wearing high heels – ouch!

'No, but if you paid attention to anyone but yourself you would have noticed me taking kick boxing lessons every Tuesday. Do keep up.' She said calmly. In a split second she'd repeated the process on Pike. Both art thieves were now rolling around on the floor, clutching their stomachs. Arabella turned towards Mrs Fairchild, who was pulling a roll of thick string from her handbag.

'But how come you're here? I thought you didn't believe us?' she asked.

'I didn't at first,' Using the heel of her shoe, Mrs Fairchild pushed Croaka flat on to her stomach. 'Do grab her arms and pull them behind her back, there's a good child,' she said to me. 'I'm going to tie her up. You, don't even think about moving.' She said sharply to Pike, who was looking scared. I dropped to the floor and did what she asked straight away. Mrs Fairchild bent down and in a trice had bound Croaka's hands together behind her back in a knot a sailor would be proud of. 'Yes, to start with, I thought you were playing a game with me, exercising your active imaginations.' She went on. 'But then little things began to catch my eye.' She pushed Pike to the floor and Arabella grabbed her arms without being asked. Mrs Fairchild produced another expert knot. 'Now do sit on their backs, dear children. It'll stop them escaping until the police get here. I phoned them when my worst fears were confirmed, just before I came and found you two. I saw the Van Gogh painting hanging off the wall with tools under it. Shocking. And I'm sorry I didn't believe you earlier.' She looked at us sadly.

'You just saved our lives, Mrs Fairchild,' I said. 'So

please don't apologise.'

Screechy police sirens suddenly filled the air outside. Croaka, who I was squashing as much as I could, began to wriggle and squirm when she heard them, but a quick, (rather hard) tap from Mrs Fairchild's shoe soon sorted her out.

In a minute, our corridor became VERY busy. One minute there was just the five of us there in the dark and the next, lights were switched on and literally HUNDREDS of police officers wearing bullet proof vests swarmed in, followed closely by Carrie, who was arm in arm with a white haired man who I recognised as Hugh Broderick.

Carrie rushed over and gave me the biggest hug. She was trembling. She hugged Arabella, then turned to look at Pike and Croaka, who were now both handcuffed and surrounded by burly, serious policemen. Pike still looked scared while Croaka looked fuming mad.

'You two ought to be ashamed of yourselves,' she said sternly. 'Deceiving pupils and teachers, then trying to rob the nation of its art. You should have chosen an honest career like the rest of us. I remember now where I've heard your names, why they sounded familiar when young Davina first told me about you. You've stolen works of art from galleries and museums around the world, haven't you? I remember seeing you on the news. The newsreader said you were two of the most wanted criminals in the world.'

'Yes, I think we'll have quite a few high up police officers from all over the globe on the phone when news of this arrest gets out,' said a big, red man. He must have been an important policeman because all other ones kept asking him questions. He turned to look at me and Arabella. 'Apologies for not believing you when you phoned.' He spoke gruffly and looked a bit embarrassed. 'It was me you spoke to. You've both done a sterling job, helping to catch this man and woman.

There'll always be a job here waiting for you on the force for when you're older – you've already proven yourselves fine detectives.'

'Thank you. But hang on a minute, did you say *man* and a woman?' I asked, feeling puzzled. I looked at Pike and Croaka. 'They are two *women*. Aren't they?'

'Of course I'm a man, you silly little worm,' Croaka yelled. 'Didn't you notice? With my deep voice and broad shoulders? The way my sister Jacinta kept calling me Chris? It stands for Christopher, not Christine. You must be even more stupid than I thought. Those women's clothes were so uncomfortable, I can't wait to put my jeans on again.'

'Here, don't you talk to my Davina like that,' Carrie said crossly. 'And I think you'll be wearing prison uniform, not jeans, where you're going. Isn't that right, Hugh?'

'Absolutely correct,' said the man with tufty white

eyebrows, who'd so far been standing next to Carrie observing everything. 'Davina and Arabella, you've done some top class detecting work. And with hardly any help, I hear.' Mrs Fairchild and the important policeman blushed red at this point. 'I thought you might want to know,' Hugh went on. 'That as soon as Carrie explained everything to me, I had some men go over to bunker thirty seven and pick up Katie Cherry and Harriet Wise. They're both being looked after in hospital now.'

'Oh thank goodness,' I said. 'Are they OK? Poor Harriet sounded very ill.'

'Harriet is diabetic, she needs to have her medicine called insulin with her at all times,' Hugh explained. 'The little she had with her when they were kidnapped soon ran out and she became very poorly, but she is being very well looked after now. The doctor I spoke to says she'll make a full recovery. They both send you two and Carrie their thanks.'

I have to go now, Diary, because Mrs Fairchild – who hasn't done any mad twirling or dancing since she got here so I think that might all be an act – says she wants to have a word with Arabella and I in private.

5.30 AM on Tuesday 1st October

Yawn, Diary...

Arabella, me, Mrs Fairchild, Carrie and Hugh (until he fell asleep on a chair in the corner) have just finished putting up the Annual Egmont Art Show in the National Gallery of Art and Design. And it looks pretty fabulous, even if I do say so myself.

That's what Mrs Fairchild wanted to talk to us about, after Croaka and Pike had been led away in shame, handcuffed and surrounded by loads of policemen. She said it would be silly to let two selfish criminals spoil such a strong artistic tradition and did we think we had enough energy left to help her put up the show? She said no problem at all if we didn't, but Arabella and I said yes, yes, yes and Carrie said she'd help as she wasn't going to let me out of her sight quite so quickly, not after everything that had happened. And Hugh said that if Carrie was helping, he would too, as she'd travelled with him to the gallery and wouldn't be able to get home if he didn't stay.

Mr Cerise, the man in charge of the gallery, arrived in a total flap ten minutes after we'd started arranging the show, at about half past one in the morning. He said a police officer had phoned him to let him know about the attempted burglary about and he was so worried he'd jumped in to his car right away and driven straight here. Arabella and I couldn't stop giggling because he was still wearing his pyjamas, which were red with a white paint brush design. After Carrie had made him

a cup of tea in the gallery kitchen and advised him to pull

himself together, Mr Cerise stopped pacing around flapping his

hands and calmed down enough to fix the painting and frame

that Croaka and Pike had tried to steal.

The art show space Egmont School had been given

was also in the Orange Room. We had two enormous bare

walls to fill with pupils work. It was MEGA exciting to think that

my painting would be on show in the same room as Vincent

Van Gogh's!

We worked on the exhibition for hours, wanting it to

look totally perfect. Mr Cerise lent us tons of spare gold and

silver picture frames that he'd stored in an upstairs cupboard,

before escaping to do some work in his office. Arabella and I

spent quite a long time matching each first year's painting to

the right sized frame. Mrs Fairchild and Carrie made a good

team, with Mrs Fairchild standing on a chair holding a hammer and nail in one hand and a frame in the other and Carrie saying, 'Up a bit, left a bit, no I mean right a bit, there – perfect.'

When they'd put my painting up, Carrie gave me a kiss and said she was very proud of me. They put Arabella's little one of a maths book next to it. The paintings did look smart all together against the deep orange wall. I couldn't wait to tell all the other first years about everything that had happened. That is if any of them except Arabella were talking to me...

Right Diary, I have to go now because Mrs Fairchild is going to drive us back to Egmont. I think I might fall asleep in her car because I'm so very, very zzzzzzzzzzzzzzzzzzz....

Thursday 3rd October

I've just had the best news, Diary!

Arabella and I have been voted in as head of year prefects! Can you imagine?! I'm so extremely excited.com.

It turns out that while we were kidnapped at the National Gallery of Art and Design, Melody overheard Cleo and Clarice giggling about what other notes they could write, pretending to be us, during dinner. She quickly told the rest of the first year and they called a meeting with Clarice and Cleo that evening and told them they'd found out about the note writing. At first Clarice and Cleo tried to deny everything but in the end they gave in and admitted it, before storming off saying they didn't want to be prefects for a bunch of losers anyway. Then, in the morning, when Arabella and I were asleep in the infirmary under Matron's watchful eye, (Mrs Fairchild was very firm about this, she said we had to rest for several hours without being disturbed) word somehow leaked out about us being kidnapped by Croaka and Pike. By the time we joined the rest of the school for lunch in the hall, everyone knew all about how we'd escaped, been chased, captured the art thieves with Mrs Fairchild and helped to display the Annual Egmont Art Show. I can't help thinking the crafty headmistress had a hand in leaking the information.

'Look, here come the heroes!' Suzie yelled as she saw us come in, rubbing our eyes. Everyone in the lunch hall broke in to applause and some people even drummed on the table with their knives and forks and stamped their feet hard on the floor, while the canaries overhead joined in by singing. Honestly, Diary, it was awesome and very noisy!

Everyone wanted to sit on our table during lunch, and people were asking so many questions.

'Is it true that Croaka was really a man?'

'Did they hurt you?'

'How did you escape?'

'Is It true that Mrs Fairchild attacked them like a ninja?'

'Did they manage to steal any art?'

We tried to answer them all as best we could and I hardly had time to eat any of my asparagus and bean wrap even though I was starving.

Near the end of lunch, Mrs Fairchild appeared, which I thought very odd because she never usually comes in to the lunch hall.

She called for quiet, then looked over at Arabella and I and smiled.

'Hello everyone,' she said. 'I have a special announcement to make, one that I usually reserve for the last assembly before half term, but as you may have heard, this has not been a typical week for many reasons.

Last night, two very brave first years, Davina Dupree and Arabella Rothsbury, saved the National Gallery of Art and Design from being robbed by two terrible art thieves. Christopher Croaka and Jacinta Pike had wormed their way in to our school by kidnapping our two excellent art teachers Katie Cherry and Harriet Wise, forcing them to write handwritten resignation letters which then arrived on my desk. They'd then turned up the day I advertised for emergency art teachers, with Christopher Croaka disguised as a woman. I regret to say I was completely deceived by them. Feeling that we needed to employ two more teachers quickly, I'm sorry to say I hired them on the spot, something that I now wish I'd never done.' She stopped for a minute, looking upset. But then her eyes twinkled again as she looked over at us.

'Davina and Arabella realised there was something

fishy about Miss Croaka and Miss Pike early on in the term,'

she went on. 'And came to tell me but I thought their story was

so fanciful I didn't believe them. So they phoned the police and

spoke to a policeman who didn't take their story seriously,

thinking it was so outlandish it must be a crank call.

To cut a long story short, Davina and Arabella turned

detectives *themselves* and found out that Katie Cherry and

Harriet Wise had been kidnapped. They even found out where

they were being held.' There were a few gasps from around

the room.

'Miss Pike and Miss Croaka,' Mrs Fairchild went on.

'Or should I say Christopher and Jacinta, realised that Davina

and Arabella knew about their plans when Davina bravely

painted a rather good picture of an art robbery for the Annual

Egmont Art Show, hoping that the shock of others knowing

about their criminal plans would stop the thieves from carrying them out.

But instead, the thieves brought the day of the Art Show forward and kidnapped Davina and Arabella. They were actually in the National Gallery of Art and Design, in the process of stealing their first painting, "Starry Night" by Vincent Van Gogh, when those two brave school girls escaped from the cupboard they'd been locked in and managed to phone Carrie Whepple, who immediately jumped in to action and got a detective friend of hers to call the police.

By that stage I had also been doing a little detecting work of my own. I'd been rather puzzled by Miss Croaka and Miss Pike's conversation as they loaded the art for the show in to their car. At first they didn't realise I was listening and I heard them talk about "picking up the little worms" before "blast off". So later that evening, after they'd driven off to put up the exhibition, I went along to their apartments and had a good snoop around. To my horror I found Katie Cherry's purse, a map of the gallery with notes about which paintings they wanted to steal all over it and worst of all a copy of Davina and Arabella's timetables.' I looked at Arabella and she shook her head. Neither of us had known anything about *that*.

'At that point, realising what a fool I'd been, I rushed over to the gallery myself and found my fears confirmed. When I arrived I saw a priceless Van Gogh painting half hanging off the wall with a bag of tools underneath it, but there was no sign of Christopher and Jacinta, or of Davina and Arabella. I immediately phoned the police, then luckily tracked the criminals down just as they'd cornered the girls. Davina and Arabella were magnificently brave as they helped me to capture and tie up the thieves. Suddenly *two* sets of police forces arrived, one called by Carrie's detective friend and one called by me. They arrested the thieves straight away. Davina and Arabella helped me put up a rather good art show, one I'm sure you'd all be very proud of.

The good news is that it seems the other first years agree with my opinion of Davina and Arabella because they've voted them in early as head of year prefects. They came to me this morning and told me and I've honestly never known a more deserving pair. Come to the front, you two, and collect your badges.'

With burning cheeks but feeling rather proud, I made my way towards Mrs Fairchild with Arabella following close behind. As we walked, the lunch hall erupted with cheers and applause, and the canaries overhead joined in, tweeting away like mad, it was TOTALLY AND UTTERLY ASTONISHING.COM! Girls we didn't even know from other years were leaning forward to pat our backs or shake our hands and Suzie Bagshaw and her friends gave us three cheers.

To top everything off, two more people arrived. It was

Katie and Harriet, I recognised them straight away from the school photos. They were both thin and pale, especially Harriet, but smiling away merrily. They were holding the prefect badges and as we went up to them they gave us ENORMOUS hugs. After all the fuss had died down, Katie told me that in a few weeks, when they're feeling strong and well enough, they're going to return to their old jobs and teach us all art. About time.com.

No one's seen Clarice or Cleo since lunch, although Melody says she thought she saw two girls with long, blonde hair heading towards a private jet on the runway. Oh well, it looks like they're not good losers! I wonder if they've got permission to just fly off...

So, Diary, I'm now lying on my bed, proudly wearing my prefect badge. Being an Egmont badge, it's made from solid gold and the word 'prefect' is written in diamonds. How grand!

It's been one whirlwind of a half term but my goodness it was exciting. Mostly. Except for being kidnapped – that was just scary. So I can safely say that I DO like it here at boarding school after all.

Anyway, Diary, I have to go now as Carrie will be arriving in a minute. Mrs Fairchild has invited her, us and Hugh and Marjorie Broderick to a slap up cream tea in her office and she says if we're lucky she might even entertain us with some salsa dancing. Whatafunnylady.com!

P.S. On the way to Mrs Fairchild's office we noticed there was a crowd round the first year's notice board, so of course we had to find out what was going on. There was a letter pinned in the centre of it from Mrs Fairchild and when I read it, my eyes nearly popped out of my head...

To the dear girls in Sapphires, Emeralds and Rubies,

Your geography teacher, Mr Fossil, and I have

organised a compulsory school trip for you all. At the beginning of next term we will travel together in private jets to the Beach of Golden Sands, fifty miles from Egmont, where a private yacht will be waiting to sail us to Ni Island, a little known sand island where hundreds of rare birds and animals live.

We will live there in luxury tents for ten days, to give you the chance to study the wildlife under Mr Fossil's tuition. I must tell you that pirates were spotted sailing close to Ni Island a few years ago, but I have been assured by the Department of the Seven Seas that they have all since been captured and imprisoned. I shall be writing to reassure your parents of the safety and educational value of the trip this evening,

Always yours truly,

Mrs Fairchild

The End

28315182R00079